August 13, 2011
To Nicholas
from Antte Teri

Stopping by Woods on a Snowy Evening

ROBERT FROST
STOPPING BY WOODS ON A SNOWY EVENING
ILLUSTRATED BY SUSAN JEFFERS

E. P. Dutton   New York

Library of Congress Cataloging in Publication Data

Frost, Robert, 1874-1963.

Stopping by woods on a snowy evening.

Summary: Illustrations of wintry scenes accompany each line
of the well-known poem.
[1. Winter—Poetry.   2. American Poetry]
I. Jeffers, Susan.   II. Title.
PZ8.3F937St   1978   811'.5'2   78-8134   ISBN: 0-525-40115-6

Published in the United States by E. P. Dutton,
a division of Penguin Books USA Inc.

Editor: Ann Durell   Designer: Riki Levinson
Printed in the U.S.A.   COBE
20 19 18 17 16

for Judes, the jewel

Whose woods these are I think I know.

His house is in the village, though;

He will not see me stopping here
To watch his woods fill up with snow.

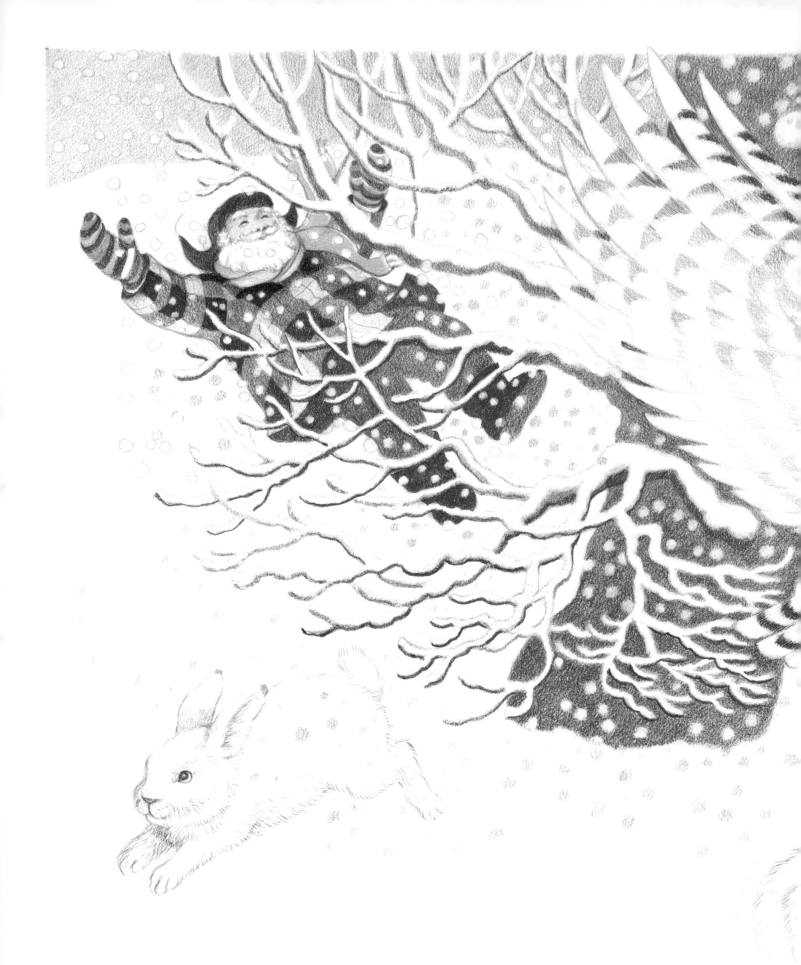

My little horse must think it queer
To stop without a farmhouse near

Between the woods and frozen lake
The darkest evening of the year.

He gives his harness bells a shake
To ask if there is some mistake.

The only other sound's the sweep

Of easy wind

and downy flake.

The woods are lovely, dark, and deep,

But I have promises to keep,

And miles to go before I sleep,

And miles to go before I sleep.

SUSAN JEFFERS says that when she was working on this book, "around my studio were the woods and animals I love to draw. Many appear in the illustrations—the birds, a deer which often fed outside my window, and a horse named Shanti."

After graduating from Pratt Institute, Ms. Jeffers worked for several publishers. "I developed a concrete knowledge of children's books and began to feel again the love I had for them as a child. As I worked on other artists' books, I became more and more eager to do my own." Her own now include *Three Jovial Huntsmen*, a Caldecott Honor Book, and *Wild Robin*.

The author's initials are hand-lettered. Other display type is photo-lettering, combining Tommy Thompson Coliseum with Trafalgar Initials. The text type is Goudy Oldstyle Alphatype. The base plate for the art was prepared with pencil and pen and ink; overlays were drawn in pencil.